Please return / renew by date shown.
You can renew it at:
norlink.norfolk.gov.uk
or by telephone: 0344 800 8006
Please have your library card & PIN ready

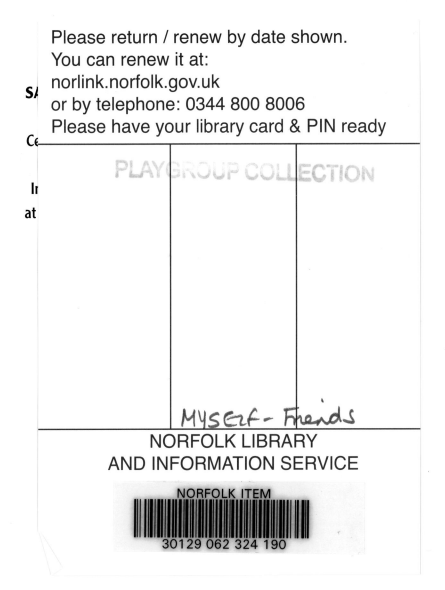

PLAYGROUP COLLECTION

MYSELF - Friends

NORFOLK LIBRARY
AND INFORMATION SERVICE

To Katherine

First published in Great Britain in 2009 and in the USA in 2010 by
Frances Lincoln Children's Books, 4 Torriano Mews,
Torriano Avenue, London NW5 2RZ

www.franceslincoln.com

First paperback published in Great Britain in 2012

A catalogue record for this book is available from the British Library.

ISBN: 978-1-84780-260-6

The illustrations in this book are lino prints

Printed in Dongguan, Guangdong, China by Toppan Leefung in June 2011.

1 3 5 7 9 8 6 4 2

Gary and Ray

Sarah Adams

F

FRANCES LINCOLN
CHILDREN'S BOOKS

Deep in an African forest there lived
a gorilla called Gary.

All the other animals had friends to play with.
But Gary was sad because he was all alone.

The elephants played together.

The monkeys hugged each other.

Even the owls were friends.

But poor Gary had no one. The children from
the nearby village were too afraid to come near.
If only Gary could tell them that he was frightened too.

At night he dreamed that fierce hunters came to take him away. But no one was there to comfort him when he woke up.

"Will anyone ever love me?" thought Gary.

Suddenly to Gary's surprise a tiny sunbird
flew into his hand.

"Aren't you scared of me?" asked Gary.

"No," answered the bird. "You looked
so unhappy, I came to say hello.
My name is Ray."

Gary and Ray were soon best friends.
They liked to dance…

Sing and

Hide-and-seek was their favourite game.
First Ray would hide...

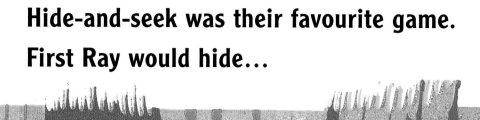

and then Gary.

Ray introduced Gary to his family.
Gary liked to watch them together
but he wished he could have a family
of his own.

Early one morning Gary woke up
to find Ray had gone.
Gary felt lonelier than ever.
He missed his little friend.

Long days passed. Then one morning Gary heard a familiar friendly sound. It was Ray!

"Come with me!" chirped Ray excitedly.

"Where are we going?" asked Gary, overjoyed to see his friend again.

"It's a surprise," said Ray.

For two days, Ray led Gary
deeper into the forest.
Then Gary stopped
in amazement.

"Gary, meet Susan,"
said Ray smiling.

Gary's heart was suddenly filled
with love and hope.
Susan gave a shy smile.
She loved Gary too.

And Gary was never lonely again.

MORE BOOKS IN PAPERBACK
FROM FRANCES LINCOLN CHILDREN'S BOOKS

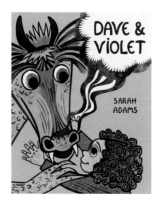

Dave and Violet
Sarah Adams

Violet thinks her best friend Dave is beautiful. But she doesn't know he is very shy. When she persuades Dave to meet her friends, he becomes nervous – and as he grows hotter with embarrassment, flames gush from his mouth. Violet's friends run away and Dave realises he is going to find it hard to fit in. But one evening his flaming breath is just what is needed to rescue a damp situation.

Batty
Sarah Dyer

No one notices Batty hanging upside down at the zoo. But trying to join in with the other animals is not for him. It's only when he returns to the bat enclosure that he makes a surprising discovery about what he is really good at. Turn the book around to see Batty's point of view, in this funny and original story by an exciting and award-winning picture book talent.

Bubble Trouble
Margaret Mahy

What a terrible thing to lose a baby brother in a bubble! Follow the hilarious efforts of Mabel and the townsfolk as they work together to save Baby – and rascal rebel Abel whose pebble and sling are ready to triple trouble! Can Mabel and friends save her brother and the day?